HiP-HoP LoLLiPoP

by **SUSAN McELROY MONTANARi**
illustrated by **BRIAN PiNKNEY**

schwartz & wade books • new york

Mama says, "Lollipop, stop!

Stop!

Jumping snapping

Nonstop."

Arms and shoulders pop 'n' lock.

Lollie's dancing **hip-hop.**

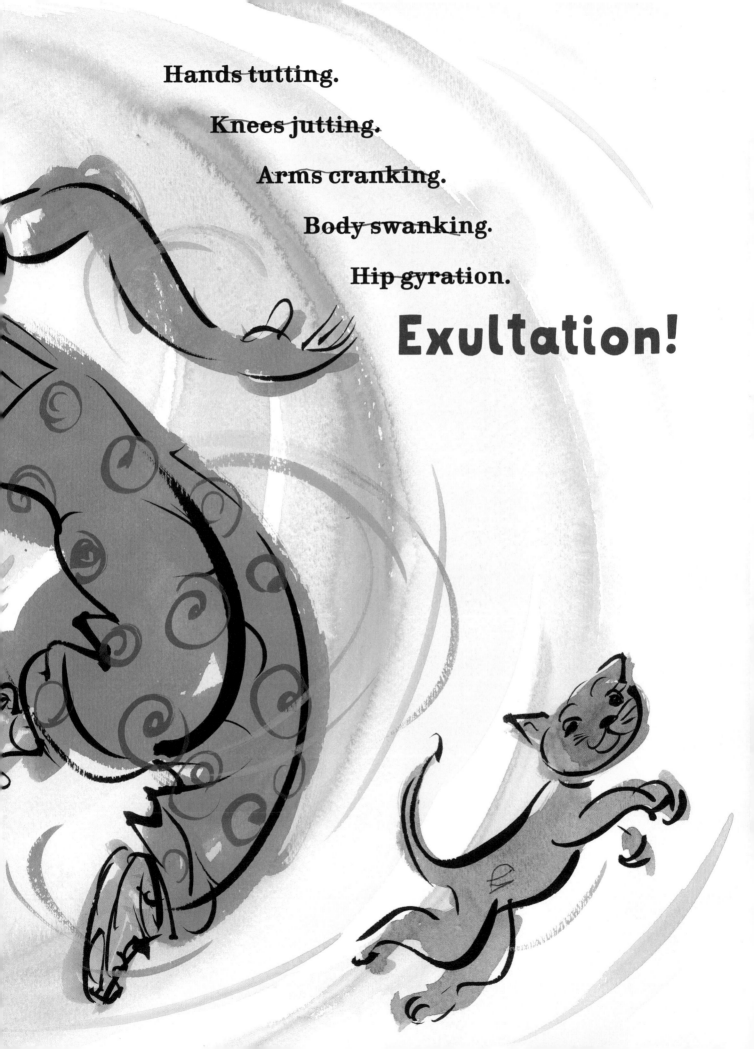

Hands tutting.

Knees jutting.

Arms cranking.

Body swanking.

Hip gyration.

Exultation!

Mama says, "Time for bed. **Bed.**"

Lollie's arms overhead.

Dancing down the long hall,

Bouncing off the tall wall.

At Big Sister's doorway,

Lollie stops to say "Hey!"

Tasha's jam is techno—

She glides heel-to-toe in *slo-mo.*

Flashing her a big grin,

Lollie's quick to jump in.

Arms and shoulders pop 'n' lock—
Sisters dancing hip-hop!

The clock upon the wall chimes.

Daddy calls, "It's bedtime!"

Teeth brushing.

Music crushing!

Bass thumping.

Shoulders pumping!

Head rotation.

Jubilation!

On the floor, Copper snores.

Lollie drops to all fours.

Boo Boo **pounces** on her back,

Curls up snug to take a nap.

Lollie yawns, rests her head,

As if the dog's a comfy bed.

Mama scoops her up high

Up into the sky.

Sky.

Then swings Lollie down low.

"In your room you go. **Go!**"

Daddy calls, **"It's fun, hon.**

But turn the music down some."

Lollie finds her pj's,

Blows kisses to the DJ,

Spins the music low.

Low.

(She can still hear it, though.)

Pulls the covers up tight,
Shouts out loud, "**Night night!**"

That's when Daddy comes in,

Turns the lights to dim.

Dim.

Leans across the big bed,

Kisses Lollie's forehead.

Sighing deeply.

Oh so sleepy.

Last rotation.

Relaxation.

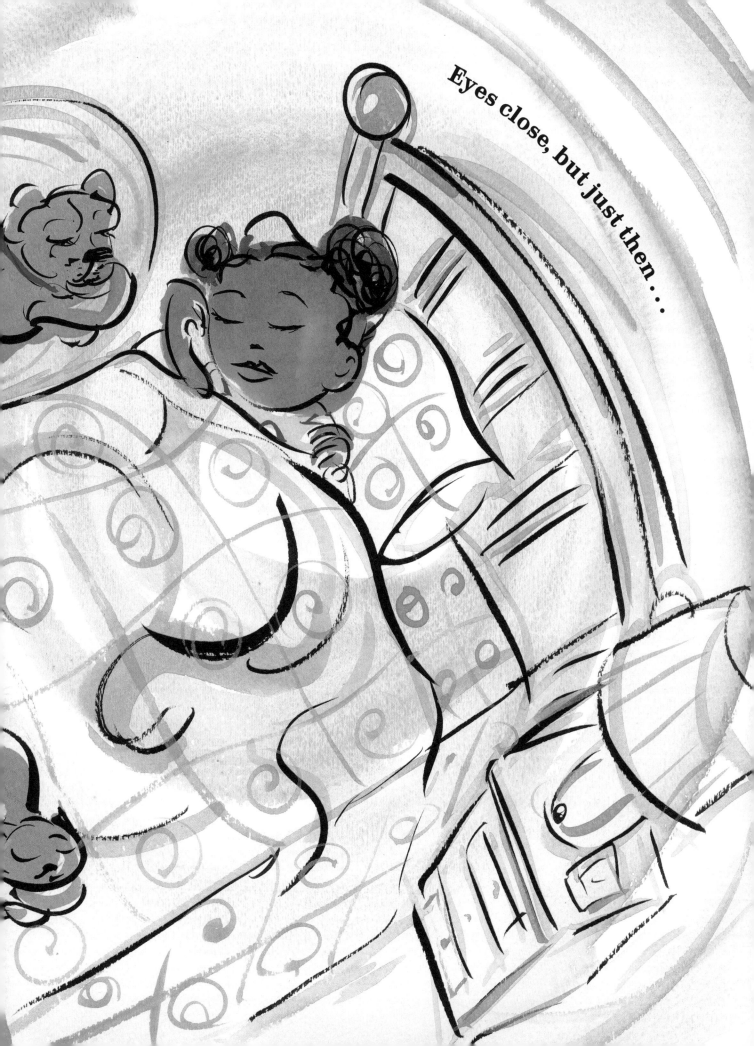

Eyes close, but just then . . .

Jumping

Snapping

Nonstop.

Lollie's **DREAMING** hip-hop!

With love to Bob and Mary Ann Grant.
Thank you for always being there! —S.M.

To Taryn —B.P.

Text copyright © 2018 by Susan McElroy Montanari

Jacket art and interior illustrations copyright © 2018 by Brian Pinkney

All rights reserved. Published in the United States by Schwartz & Wade Books, an imprint of Random House Children's Books,
a division of Penguin Random House LLC, New York.

Schwartz & Wade Books and the colophon are trademarks of Penguin Random House LLC.

Visit us on the Web! rhcbooks.com

Educators and librarians, for a variety of teaching tools, visit us at RHTeachersLibrarians.com

Library of Congress Cataloging-in-Publication Data is available upon request.

ISBN 978-1-101-93482-1 (trade) —ISBN 978-1-101-93483-8 (lib. bdg.) —ISBN 978-1-101-93484-5 (ebook)

The text of this book is set in ParmaTypewriterPro.

The illustrations were rendered in watercolor and India ink on Strathmore watercolor paper.

MANUFACTURED IN CHINA

2 4 6 8 10 9 7 5 3 1

First Edition